D1017032

Dear Parents:

Congratulations! Your child is taking the first steps on an exciting journey. The destination? Independent reading!

STEP INTO READING® will help your child get there. The program offers five steps to reading success. Each step includes fun stories and colorful art or photographs. In addition to original fiction and books with favorite characters, there are Step into Reading Non-Fiction Readers, Phonics Readers and Boxed Sets, Sticker Readers, and Comic Readers—a complete literacy program with something to interest every child.

Learning to Read, Step by Step!

Ready to Read   Preschool–Kindergarten
• **big type and easy words** • **rhyme and rhythm** • **picture clues**
For children who know the alphabet and are eager to begin reading.

Reading with Help   Preschool–Grade 1
• **basic vocabulary** • **short sentences** • **simple stories**
For children who recognize familiar words and sound out new words with help.

Reading on Your Own   Grades 1–3
• **engaging characters** • **easy-to-follow plots** • **popular topics**
For children who are ready to read on their own.

Reading Paragraphs   Grades 2–3
• **challenging vocabulary** • **short paragraphs** • **exciting stories**
For newly independent readers who read simple sentences with confidence.

Ready for Chapters   Grades 2–4
• **chapters** • **longer paragraphs** • **full-color art**
For children who want to take the plunge into chapter books but still like colorful pictures.

STEP INTO READING® is designed to give every child a successful reading experience. The grade levels are only guides; children will progress through the steps at their own speed, developing confidence in their reading.

Remember, a lifetime love of reading starts with a single step!

For my mom, who I
believe can do anything
—A. J.

Step into Reading, Random House, and the Random House colophon are registered trademarks of Random House LLC.

Visit us on the Web!
StepIntoReading.com
randomhousekids.com

Educators and librarians, for a variety of teaching tools, visit us at RHTeachersLibrarians.com

ISBN 978-0-7364-3341-9 (trade) — ISBN 978-0-7364-8223-3 (lib. bdg.)
ISBN 978-0-7364-3340-2 (ebook)

Printed in the United States of America

10 9 8 7 6 5 4 3

DISNEY PRINCESS

A Princess CAN!

By Apple Jordan

Illustrated by Francesco Legramandi
and Gabriella Matta

Random House 🏠 New York

Today is game day.
Merida has to play
a new sport.

She is afraid
she will not win.

Her father helps
her practice.

She can do it!

The first game starts.
Merida throws the ball
far.

She does not win.

But Merida is happy.

She tried her best.

Merida did it!

Rapunzel loves
to draw and paint.

The King asks Rapunzel
to paint a mural.
It is a big job.
She can do it!

First she draws.

Then she paints.

Rapunzel works hard.

At last the mural is done.

The King loves it!
The Queen loves it!
The whole kingdom
loves it!

Rapunzel did it!

Tiana owns a café.
She is the boss.

Tiana is writing
a speech.
She will talk to kids
about her café.

Tiana practices,
and practices,
and practices.

On the big day,
Tiana is scared.
She can do it!

Tiana did it!

31901061354777